The Santa Secret

by **Carol Wallace**

illustrated by
Steve Björkman

Holiday House / New York

Reading Level: 2.7

Text copyright © 2007 by Carol Wallace
Illustrations copyright © 2007 by Steve Björkman
All Rights Reserved
Printed and Bound in China
www.holidayhouse.com
First Edition
1 3 5 7 9 10 8 6 4 2

Library of Congress Cataloging-in-Publication Data
Wallace, Carol, 1948-
The Santa secret / by Carol Wallace ; illustrated by Steve Björkman. — 1st ed.
p. cm.
Summary: With the help of the family bloodhound, a little girl's secret
Christmas wish, known only to Santa, finally comes true.

ISBN-13: 978-0-8234-2022-3 (hardcover)
ISBN-13: 978-0-8234-2126-8 (paperback)

[1. Christmas—Fiction. 2. Family life—Fiction. 3. Santa Claus—Fiction.
4. Bloodhound—Fiction. 5. Dogs—Fiction.] I. Björkman, Steve, ill. II. Title.

PZ7.W15473San 2007
[E]—dc22
2006019532

To Kaden Keith
and William Keith
C. W.

For Alex Uhl,
whose Whale of a Tale
Children's Bookshoppe
has inspired so many
S. B.

Contents

1. Kari Won't Tell   6

2. Santa Land   12

3. Too Late   17

4. Santa's Surprise   20

Chapter 1
Kari Won't Tell

D. B. stretched out on the porch.

His jowls hung over his front paws.

He whiffed the country air.

It was almost Christmas.

The bloodhound sat up.

His ears perked at the voices

from the house.

"Kari, it's almost Christmas.
You have to tell us what
you really want," Mama said.
"Santa knows." Kari smiled.
"Do you want clothes? New shoes?"
"New clothes would be okay,"
Kari said.

"You may get socks!" Kevin said.

Mike laughed.

"You need a backup plan.

Just in case there's a mistake.

One time I got

red cowboy boots."

"Now, Mike.

That wasn't Santa's mistake.

Great-grandma Jenkins

can't hear very well.

When you said Ladders and Chutes,

what she heard was bright red boots."

"Maybe a doll?" Daddy asked.

"Santa knows what I want."

"Have you *told* Santa what you want?
I forgot to tell Santa I wanted a bike.
I got underwear," Mike warned.

"You might get something really weird,"
Kevin agreed.

"*You* don't understand," Kari said.

"Santa already knows what I want."

Daddy walked over by Mama.

"Let's go to the mall," he whispered.

"We'll visit Santa."

"Good idea," Mama said.

"Maybe she'll tell him."

The next day,

D. B. watched his family

pile into the car.

As they drove away,

he went to his doghouse.

He hopped up on the roof.

Then he jumped to the top

of the shed.

Finally he leaped to the roof

of the house.

There he sat down beside the chimney.

He watched the car drive away.

Chapter 2
Santa Land

The roar of the car woke D. B.

He was waiting on the porch

when his family got out of the car.

D. B. followed Kari into the house.

"Well, that was fun!" Mike said.

"I'm glad my friends didn't see me

at Santa Land."

D. B. perked his ears.

He plopped down on his bed

near the fireplace.

"That was so much fun." Mama giggled.

"What did everyone tell Santa?"

"He knows I want a new fishing rod
and reel." Daddy grinned.

"Did I have to have
my picture taken on his lap?"

"Mike, what did you tell Santa?"
Mama asked.

"I told him I needed more cars
for my collection," Mike said.

"What did you tell him
you wanted, Mama?"
"I told him I want my children
to get along for a whole year."
Mama smiled.
"Kevin, what did you tell Santa?"
Daddy asked.
"I told him I want basketball shoes.
My old ones are pretty smelly."

"Kari, what did you tell Santa?"

"I told him that my family should get
everything they want this year."

Then everyone stared at Kari.

"That's very sweet, dear.
But what is the special thing
you want just for yourself?"

"It's Santa's secret." Kari grinned.

"Daddy and I are going to wrap
some presents. Talk to your sister."
Mama winked at Kevin.
"We know that you think Santa
knows what you want for Christmas.
But you have to *tell* someone
so he can hear you."
"Santa knows!" Kari smiled.

Chapter 3
Too Late

D. B. followed Mama and Daddy
to the car.

He whiffed the breeze.

He went to the chimney.

D. B. sniffed and sniffed.

"What do you think Kari wants?"
Mama asked.

"I don't know,
but I do hope Santa really knows.

It's Christmas Eve.

It's too late to get anything else."

Daddy shook his head.

That night when the lights went off,

D. B. climbed up on the doghouse.

Then he leaped onto the shed.

Finally he jumped up

on top of the house.

D. B. stared up at the sky.

Stars twinkled back at him.

He wondered about Santa.

Mama said you have to be asleep

before Santa would come.

D. B. hoped that Santa knew
what Kari wanted.
D. B. climbed down from the roof.
He took his place on the front porch.
He listened to the sounds of the night.
He listened for Santa.

Chapter 4
Santa's Surprise

Just as the sun peeked
over the horizon,
D. B. hopped off the porch.
D. B. climbed to the roof again.
He sniffed and sniffed.
He could not smell Santa.
He could not smell anything.
Maybe Santa forgot to come.
D. B. perked his ears.
The wind was still.
There was a chill in the air.

D. B. went to the door.

"Let me in," he howled.

"It's getting cold."

"What's going on, D. B.? Come on."

The dog rushed in

and sniffed each gift.

Then he lay down by the fireplace.

"D. B., guard the door.

Keep the kids out," Daddy teased.

Mama put more gifts around the tree.

Daddy checked the Christmas stockings.

D. B. looked at the gifts.

He sniffed at the pile of presents.

"Okay, D. B. Get the kids,"

Mama called.

The big dog walked to the hall.

"Woof! Woof!" he barked.

The door to the boys' room flew open.

The boys looked around.

"Let's get Kari."

They shoved open her door.

When they came out,

Kari was in their arms.

"Mama! Daddy! Help!" Kari called.

"Put her down, boys.

It's time to open your presents."

Kevin and Mike read each tag.

They made a pile in front of Kari.

Each boy had a pile too.

D. B. even had two presents,

a box of dog treats

and a chewy bone.

D. B. munched on the bone.

Soon the room was filled
with paper and boxes.
Mike put his cars in a big circle
in front of him.

Kevin stacked his clothes in a big pile.

New basketball shoes were on top.

Daddy put his fishing stuff
in a new tackle box.

Mama had a new bathrobe
and slippers.

She also had a shiny new ring.

Kari was very quiet.

She had a pair of jeans
and two new shirts.

She had a baby doll in a stroller.

Kari played with a new game.

"Did Santa bring you
what you wanted?" Daddy asked.

Everyone got quiet.

"Not yet. But he knows what I want."
Kari looked around at her family.
The house creaked as a big gust
of wind shook the whole house.
"That blue northerner is finally here,"
Daddy exclaimed.
"Do you think it will snow?"
Kari's eyes brightened.
"I guess that's what
D. B. has been looking for.
He's been whiffing around
everywhere." Kevin laughed.

"I saw him on the roof," Mike said.

Everyone looked at D. B.

The dog chewed his toy.

"Hmm. He was on the roof?"

"He does that all the time.

He jumps from his doghouse

to the shed, then up

on the roof," Mike said.

"You don't say. That's a pretty
good trick for a big, old dog."
Daddy rubbed his head.
D. B. suddenly perked his ears.
A small scratching sound
came to his ears.

A strange smell came too.
The dog hopped to his feet
and followed his nose.
The noise seemed
to be near
the fireplace.

"Let's have a fire, Dad," Kevin said.
The scratching was loud.
Why couldn't his family hear it?
D. B. barked.
Daddy knelt down by the fireplace.
D. B. barked again.
Daddy stuffed paper and twigs
into the fireplace.

D. B. caught Daddy's sleeve
in his teeth.
"What is wrong with you, dog?"
Mama asked.

D. B. pointed to the fireplace.
He barked and barked.

"There must be something in there,"
Kari said.

Daddy pulled out the paper and twigs.

He peered up into the chimney.

"I think you're right."

Daddy reached into the opening.

"Mew. Mew."

A small sound came from the opening.

A kitten covered in gray soot

was in Daddy's hands.

"See, I told you."

Kari hugged the kitten.

"*Owww,*" D. B. howled.

Mama, Daddy, Kevin,
and Mike stared.

"See, Santa knows." Kari smiled.
The kitten purred
as Kari brushed away the ashes.
"Santa did know."

D. B. slipped out the door.

He raced to the top of his doghouse.

He climbed to the shed.

He jumped to the roof.

He sniffed all around the chimney.

D. B. was a bloodhound.

His nose was better than

any other dog's in the world.

There was no smell of Santa.

No smell of people.

No smell of kitten.

D. B. couldn't figure it out.

He *did* figure out that Kari was right.

It was Santa's secret!